ENGLA

LEGEND

1. LONDON
2. SALISBURY CATHEDRAL
3. STONEHEDGE
4. BRISTOL
5. GLASTONBURY RUINS
6. AVENBURY STONES
7. WOODSTOCK

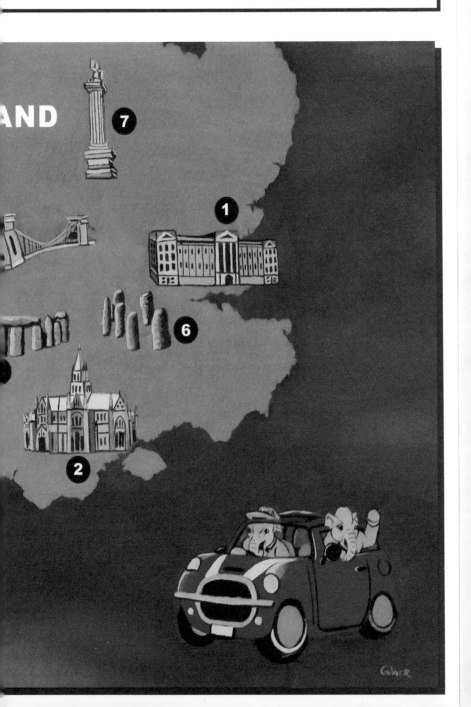

An Elephant Family Adventure:

The Elephants Tour England

By
Beverly Eschberger

Illustrated By
Jim Gower

Praise for *The Elephants Visit London*!

New Mexico Book Award Finalist, 2008

Children's Bookwatch: Midwest Book Review

The Elephants Visit London is a delightful and inexpensive treat for young readers who have just discovered the joy of chapter books. Following the Elephant Family (two parents and their twin children Harold and Penelope - all of the bipedal elephants dressed in nice travel clothes) during their trip to London. The Elephants Visit London shows an elephant's-eye view of historic buildings, traditional English food, and the Natural History Museum. But when the twins suddenly go missing from the museum, detectives from Scotland Yard are set on the case! The last few pages offer lists to help young readers reacquaint themselves with British English terms mentioned in the book, such as "telephone call box" (telephone booth). A scattering of simple black-and-white illustrations round out this wonderful book, fun to read in its own right and especially recommended to help prepare young people for the culture shock of visiting London and England.

Sabra Brown Steinsiek

The Elephants Visit London is a delightful read for children and the adults who read it to them. Every child will giggle at the possibility of a trench coat and hat being enough to disguise an elephant! They'll understand that only adults are too blinded by what they see to look beyond to the reality that lies within. Eschberger has incorporated a lot of history and sight-seeing in a witty story. As a former children's librarian, I'd be happy to hand this book to one of my patrons. Bring on the next Adventure...and don't forget the peas!

Mom's Choice Awards ® Silver Award Winner

The Mom's Choice Awards® honors excellence in family-friendly media, products and services. An esteemed panel of judges includes education, media and other experts as well as parents, children, librarians, performing artists, producers, medical and business professionals, authors, scientists and others. Parents and educators look for the Mom's Choice Awards® seal in selecting quality materials and products for children and families. This book has been honored by this distinguished award.

Books By Beverly Eschberger

Currently Available:

The Elephants Visit London
The Elephants Tour England

Other adventures with the Elephant Family soon to be published by Artemesia Publishing:

The Elephants in the Land of Enchantment
The Elephants Visit the City of Light

ISBN13: 978-1-932926-29-3

Artemesia Publishing, LLC
9 Mockingbird Hill Rd
Tijeras, New Mexico 87059
info@artemesiapublishing.com
www.apbooks.net

Library of Congress Cataloging-in-Publication Data

Eschberger, Beverly Sue, 1968-
  The Elephants tour England / by Beverly Eschberger ; illustrated by
Jim Gower.
       p. cm. -- (An Elephant family adventure)
Summary: Ambassador Elephant and his family set out on a tour of
southern England, but ten-year-old twins Harold and Penelope board
the wrong bus and spend a day with a group of French students, while
their parents frantically search for them.
  ISBN 978-1-932926-29-3 (pbk.)
  1. England, Southern--Description and travel--Juvenile fiction. [1.
England, Southern--Description and travel--Fiction. 2. Bus travel--
Fiction. 3. Lost children--Fiction. 4. Elephants--Fiction.] I. Gower, Jim,
ill. II. Title.
  PZ7.E74465Eke 2009
  [Fic]--dc22
  2008039294

First Printing

An Elephant Family Adventure:
The Elephants Tour England
By
Beverly Eschberger

Illustrated By
Jim Gower

Kinkajou Press
Albuquerque, New Mexico
www.apbooks.net

To my husband Geoff, who has always supported me in everything that I have wanted to do.

Table of Contents

Chapter One

Holiday Plans

Once upon a time, a family of elephants lived in London. They had just moved to London from Elephas. Which is a small country in Africa.

Mr. Elephant had been named as an Ambassador to England. Mrs. Elephant helped her husband to be the Ambassador. She was also an artist who loved to paint and make statues.

Mr. and Mrs. Elephant had two children named Harold and Penelope. Harold and Penelope were twins and were ten years old. They went to school in London,

where they had many friends.

Penelope was the smartest student in their class. She planned to be a paleontologist when she grew up.

Penelope loved to read books about dinosaurs and other extinct animals. But she did not just like books about dinosaurs. She loved to read any book about any subject.

Harold was not as good a student as Penelope. He liked to spend his time playing games with his friends. His favorite games were those he made up with his toy soldiers.

Harold had a large collection of toy soldiers. He was always careful to save his pocket money. Then he could add new soldiers to his collection.

Harold wanted to be an astronaut when he grew up. Harold and Penelope's teacher was named Miss Wren. She often reminded Harold, "Now, Harold. You must study harder if you want to travel into space. You will need better grades in math and science."

Before they had moved to London, Mr. Elephant gathered his family together. He warned them, "In Elephas, it is not unusual to see elephants. But elephants are not very common in London"

"People might become afraid if they see an elephant

in London. So we must always wear disguises while we are there," he added.

Mr. and Mrs. Elephant wore raincoats and carried umbrellas. Harold and Penelope wore school uniforms. When they wore their costumes, they looked like an ordinary English family.

The Elephant family had lived in London for a short time. Mr. and Mrs. Elephant wanted to take a short holiday.

Mrs. Elephant telephoned a travel agency. She booked four tickets on a three-day trip. They would see famous sites in southern England.

Early Friday morning, the Elephants left the Elephas Embassy. They squeezed into a taxicab that took them to Victoria Coach Station.

Mrs. Elephant led her family to their tour coach. She said to the coach driver, "I have tickets for four. The name is Elefant. E-L-E-F-A-N-T."

When Harold and Penelope had first heard this spelling, they were confused. Penelope had asked her father, "Daddy," she had said. "Why did you spell our name Elefant with an F? Instead of with a PH?"

Her father had replied, "This is part of our disguise.

What would people guess if they met a family named Elephant?"

Now, Harold and Penelope found it funny when their parents used this false spelling. It kept people from becoming suspicious that there were elephants around. They began to giggle, but Mrs. Elephant shushed them.

"Good morning, Mrs. Elefant. My name is Colin," said the coach driver. He looked at his clipboard. "I have your family listed right here. Hmmm, Elefant... Elefant... That is an unusual name...Is it French?" asked Colin.

"No," said Mrs. Elephant. She and her family squeezed into the coach. They were very careful to tiptoe. The Elephants took seats in the back of the coach. They wore their disguises. None of the other passengers realized there were elephants on the coach.

The Roman Baths

The tour coach set off for the city of Bath. A tall lady who wore her hair in a bun stood up.

"My name is Miss Abigail," she said. "And I will be your tour guide during this trip. You can always find me by looking for my flag."

She held up a small Union Flag. She began to tell them the history of the city of Bath.

"The city of Bath was founded almost 3000 years ago. It was built around five natural hot springs," began Miss Abigail. "The area was a holy site for the Celtic

people. They worshipped a goddess named Sulis."

Harold and Penelope were both sleepy from waking up early. They both fell asleep during the drive. Mr. and Mrs. Elephant listened carefully to Miss Abigail's stories about Bath.

Colin parked the coach at the Roman Baths. Mrs. Elephant woke up Harold and Penelope. They went into the Baths and out onto the terrace. They could see Bath Abbey close by.

There were statues on the terrace above the large bath. When Harold and Penelope saw the statues, they cried out in joy.

"Look, look, at his sword and helmet," cried Harold.

"Look at her funny hair!" laughed Penelope.

"Look at the water," Harold pointed. "It's green! What is wrong with it?"

"It's from the natural minerals in the water," said Miss Abigail. "Different minerals give it different colors."

"Well, it is still pretty weird," said Harold.

Mr. Elephant was interested in the history of the baths. Mrs. Elephant was interested in the statues and wall carvings.

"I have so many ideas for artwork. I can hardly wait

to work on them," said Mrs. Elephant.

Miss Abigail held up her Union Flag so everyone could find her. She led them around the Baths and told them about the Romans.

Harold and Penelope enjoyed listening to Miss Abigail. And seeing the ancient things that had been discovered.

There was a model that Harold really liked. It showed what the Baths would have looked like during Roman times. Harold decided to build a model when he returned to London. It would be great for his toy soldiers.

Harold asked Penelope, "Are you certain you want to become a paleontologist? Maybe it would be more fun to be an archaeologist. Then you could study all these ancient artifacts. Instead of some dusty old bones. And you can build models, too!"

Penelope replied, "Maybe I can be both. I could be a paleontologist and an archaeologist. Then I could study mummies and other neat things. As well as dinosaurs."

One of the rooms was called a caldarium. Miss Abigail explained that the Romans kept fires burning under the stone floors. This made the room very hot for people who were taking baths.

"How interesting!" said Mrs. Elephant. "How

clever of the Romans to think of that idea!"

"Hmmmph," said Mr. Elephant. "I am certain elephants thought of that well before the Romans. Elephants have always been much smarter than humans."

After they toured the baths, the Elephants visited the Gift Shop. There were Roman bath salts, oil, and soap that smelled like lavender. Mrs. Elephant bought some for herself and Penelope.

Harold used his pocket money to buy Roman toy soldiers. They would be fun to add to his collection.

It was time for a traditional English lunch. The tour group went to a local pub. Everyone ordered fish and chips. And cups of tea with milk and sugar.

The Elephants were very pleased that their meals were served with peas. Because (as you may have heard before) elephants are very fond of peas.

Chapter Three

Bath Abbey

After their lunch, the tour group walked to Bath Abbey. They walked around the church looking at the stone carvings and stained glass. Miss Abigail talked about the history of the Abbey.

There were wooden carvings on the choir pews. Harold pointed at a carving. "Miss Abigail," he said, "That looks like a dragon."

"You are right, Harold," said Miss Abigail. "We will

see lots of carvings on church choir pews. We will see dragons, griffins, dogs, and other animals."

"Wow," said Harold. "I can hardly wait to see more dragons!"

Penelope was excited to see ruins of an ancient church. It was a thousand years old! Bath Abbey had been built on top of it.

After they visited the Abbey, it was time for tea. Miss Abigail took them to the Pump House in the Baths.

Everyone ordered Bath Buns and Sally Lunn buns. And cups of tea with milk and sugar.

The waiter offered everyone a drink called Spa Water. It was water that came from the spring in the Baths.

He told them, "The Victorians liked to drink it. They thought it was good for their health."

Mr. and Mrs. Elephant and Harold all tasted the Spa Water. But Penelope refused to drink any.

"It smells funny, Daddy," said Penelope. She wrinkled her trunk.

Then Miss Abigail led them through the city of Bath. She held her Union Flag high.

"During the 18th century, Bath became well known," said Miss Abigail. "People who lived in London liked to

spend their holidays here. We will see some famous places that were built at this time."

They visited a market. Mrs. Elephant bought a bag of black currant tea. She planned to serve it at the Elephas Embassy.

Harold and Penelope bought some sweets for themselves. And to share with their friends back at school.

Miss Abigail led them through the Parade Gardens and across Pulteney Bridge. There were shops along the bridge. Harold and Penelope bought some old maps in one shop.

"I want to hang this map in my bedroom," said Harold. He held up an old map of England. "Now I will know where famous battles were fought."

They saw many beautiful old buildings in Bath. After all the walking, everyone was very hungry. Miss Abigail took them to a nice pub for dinner.

Mr. Elephant ordered fish and chips. Mrs. Elephant ordered Shepherd's Pie. Penelope ordered Cornish pasty.

And Harold ordered Bangers and Mash. (He knew that they were not really firecrackers. But he kept hoping that maybe, someday…)

The Elephants were pleased that their meals were

served with peas. Because (as it is well known) elephants are very fond of peas.

Mrs. Elephant, Harold, and Penelope drank tea with milk and sugar. Mr. Elephant drank a glass of cider. It made him feel a little sleepy.

Luckily, they were staying in a hotel next to the pub. So they did not have too far to walk.

The Elephants rode the lift to their room on the top floor. Mr. Elephant said, "Remember we are on the top floor. So we must be very careful to always tiptoe. Otherwise, people might guess elephants are in the hotel."

The Elephants each took a bath. They changed into their pajamas, and brushed their teeth. Mr. and Mrs. Elephant tucked Harold and Penelope into their beds. And kissed them both goodnight.

The Elephants all went to sleep. Mr. Elephant dreamed about elephants building the Roman Baths. Mrs. Elephant dreamed about making Roman sculptures.

Penelope dreamed about finding dinosaur skeletons in Roman ruins. This pleased Penelope. She was able to enjoy both paleontology and archaeology at the same time.

Harold dreamed that he was a Roman soldier. He

was in the ancient city of Bath. He got to wear armor and a helmet. And carry a spear and sword. This made Harold very happy.

Stonehenge

The next morning, Mrs. Elephant woke up Harold and Penelope. "It is time to get dressed in your school uniforms. We are visiting Stonehenge today.

"Mummy," said Penelope. "I don't feel very good. My tummy hurts."

"Oh, my poor baby," said Mrs. Elephant. She remembered the sweets that Harold and Penelope had bought. "Did you eat too many sweets last night before bed?"

"I only ate a few," said Penelope. She knew she had

eaten more candy than she should have.

"Well, get dressed," said Mrs. Elephant. She patted Penelope's head. "We will go downstairs to the hotel café for breakfast. Maybe you will feel better after some tea and toast.

So Penelope drank a cup of tea. The rest of the Elephant family ordered Full English Breakfasts. The Elephants were very fond of Full English Breakfasts.

They were very happy to see everything on their plates. There were eggs, sausages, bacon, baked beans, tomatoes, mushrooms, and black pudding.

The Elephants squeezed into the tour coach with the rest of the group. Harold and Penelope took a nap as the coach drove to Salisbury Plain.

Miss Abigail told stories about what they would see at Stonehenge. And in the city of Salisbury.

The tour coach parked at Stonehenge. Mrs. Elephant woke up Harold and Penelope. "It is time to wake up, children. Do you feel better now, Penelope?"

Penelope sat up and rubbed her eyes. "Mummy, my tummy still hurts," said Penelope.

Harold sat up and rubbed his eyes, too. "My tummy hurts, too, Mummy," said Harold.

"Oh, my poor babies," said Mrs. Elephant. "You

two must have caught something at school."

"They have been cooped up in this coach too long," said Mr. Elephant. "Maybe a walk in the fresh air will make them feel better."

"Perhaps it will," said Mrs. Elephant. She was still very worried about her children's health.

The Elephants got off the coach with Miss Abigail and the others. They walked through the tunnel to the Stonehenge monument.

Mrs. Elephant clapped her hands. "Oh, it is so beautiful!" she cried out. "I am so glad that I have my sketchbook!"

"Hmmph," said Mr. Elephant. "It is not as big as I expected."

Miss Abigail told them about the history of Stonehenge. "First there was a wood circle here. The stone circle was built between 2500 and 1100 B.C.E. That is over 3,000 years ago! Parts of it are even older than the Egyptian Pyramids."

"Some of the stones came from as far away as Wales! This was over 250 miles away. This tells us how important it was to the people who built it."

"Now, if you will all follow me," continued Miss Abigail. "We will walk around the monument." She held her Union Flag high and waved it.

Mrs. Elephant looked at her children. Harold and Penelope were walking slowly and rubbing their tummies. "My poor babies," said Mrs. Elephant. "Do you both still feel sick?"

Harold and Penelope both nodded.

"Why don't you lie down in the coach?" asked Mrs. Elephant. She felt their foreheads for a fever.

"When the tour is finished, we will ask the driver to stop. Then we can buy some tummy medicine," said Mrs. Elephant.

"Okay," said Harold and Penelope quietly. They both walked slowly back to the parking lot. And climbed the steps of the empty tour coach. They went to the back of the bus. They lay down, and quickly fell asleep again.

Chapter Five

Missing!

Mr. and Mrs. Elephant walked back to the parking lot. They carried the gifts they had bought at the gift shop. They talked about the things they had learned during their tour.

"I am certain it was built by elephants," said Mr. Elephant. "Only elephants could have been strong enough to move those heavy stones."

"And only elephants could use it as a calendar." said

Mrs. Elephant.

"I wish we could visit other places here," said Mr. Elephant.

"Yes," said Mrs. Elephant. "Penelope and Harold are interested in archaeology. They would both like to see the burial mounds."

"Maybe Harold will decide to be an archaeologist. Instead of an astronaut," said Mr. Elephant.

"He always gets good grades in history," added Mrs. Elephant. "His toy soldiers have taught him a lot."

They reached their tour coach. Mrs. Elephant stopped to speak to Colin the driver.

"Please, could you stop at a chemist's before we go to Salisbury Cathedral? My children both have tummy aches. And I want to buy some medicine for them."

"Certainly, Mrs. Elefant," said Colin. "But, where are your children?" he asked.

"Why, they are on the coach. They are taking a nap," said Mrs. Elephant.

"That is not possible," said Colin. "While everyone was at Stonehenge, I took the coach to buy petrol. There is no one on the coach now."

"Oh, no," cried Mrs. Elephant, "That is not possible!" She squeezed onto the coach. And tiptoed quickly to the back. She looked everywhere for Harold and Penelope.

"They are missing," said Mrs. Elephant when she returned. "But we sent them back here to take a nap."

Colin removed his cap and scratched his head, "Maybe they got on another coach by mistake," he said.

"Yes," said Mr. Elephant, "Let's look on the other coaches here. Maybe Harold and Penelope are on one of them."

Miss Abigail joined Mr. and Mrs. Elephant and Colin. They went to the other coaches in the parking lot. They looked for Harold and Penelope and spoke to the drivers. But none of the other drivers had seen their children.

Then they spoke to the driver of the very last coach. He asked them, "Hmmm, what did your children look like?"

"Er, um," said Mr. Elephant. He knew he could not say his children looked like elephants. "They had rather large noses, and rather large ears."

"They were both wearing school uniforms," said Mrs. Elephant. She wept into her large handkerchief.

"Hmmm, I saw two children get onto a coach. It was from the same tour company as your coach. They

were wearing school uniforms."

"A larger group of children got on the same coach later. I wondered why the first two children had come back so much earlier."

"That must be Harold and Penelope!" cried Mr. and Mrs. Elephant.

"Which coach did they get on?" asked Mr. Elephant.

"It has already left with all the children," said the driver.

"Oh, no," cried Mrs. Elephant, "I will never see my babies again!"

"Do not worry, Mrs. Elefant," said Colin. "We know they got on a coach from our company. We will drive to Salisbury and call the tour company. They will tell us where your children are."

So Colin drove to Salisbury. He took Miss Abigail and the group to Salisbury Cathedral. He then drove Mr. and Mrs. Elephant to the coach center. Then he telephoned the tour company.

"Do not worry Mrs. Elefant," said Colin. "The company thinks your children are with a group of French students. They are visiting from Paris. Their coach left while your group was visiting Stonehenge."

"But where are they now?" asked Mr. Elephant.

"The French students are at Salisbury Cathedral right now," said Colin. "We will just drive back there and find them."

"Oh, thank goodness!" said Mrs. Elephant. She felt much better.

Chapter Six

Parlez-vous français?

Harold opened his eyes. His tummy felt much better after his nap. He sat up and stretched. Then he looked around for his mother. He did not need any tummy medicine any more.

But Harold did not see his parents. Instead, he saw two boys he did not know. They were looking at him and Penelope.

"*Bonjour,*" said one of the boys. "*Parlez-vous français?*"

Harold was confused. He reached over to Penelope and shook her awake. "Penelope," said Harold. "I don't think we are in England any more."

Penelope sat up, rubbed her eyes, and stretched. "Oh, Harold, why did you wake me up?" asked Penelope. "I was having such a lovely dream. I was dancing around Stonehenge in a beautiful white dress."

Harold pointed at the two children sitting in front of him. Penelope then noticed that there were more children.

"*Ah, bonjour,*" said a girl in front of Penelope. She had a thick French accent. "You are awake, *non?*"

"Uh, *oui,*" said Penelope, uncertainly.

"It is so nice to meet you," continued the girl. "*Je m'appelle Thérèse-Anne. Et vous êtes éléphants.*"

Harold and Penelope had just begun to study French. So they understood enough to know Thérèse-Anne realized they were elephants.

"*Ah, non,*" said Harold. "*Nous ne sommes pas éléphants. Je…je…je* just have a very big nose."

"And big ears, *aussi,*" piped up Penelope.

"*Ah, non,*" said a boy who sat in front of Harold.

"I know what an elephant looks like. And you two are elephants."

"You are not afraid that we are elephants?" asked Harold.

"You are not going to panic?" asked Penelope.

"Do not be so silly. Panic, *pourquoi? Je m'appelle Jean-Claude.* What is your name?" asked the boy.

"Uh, *je m'appelle Harold. Et c'est ma soeur Penelope,*" said Harold. He was trying to remember enough French to introduce himself and his sister.

"My name is Marie," said another girl. "I must remind my classmates that we are here to practice our English. And our teacher wants us to speak only English."

"That's good," said Harold. "I can never remember if things are *le* or *la.*"

"*Il est très stupide,*" said Penelope. She was showing off. The other children laughed. Harold scowled at her.

"But you weren't in our tour group from London," said Harold.

"You must have gotten onto our *autobus* by mistake," said Jean-Claude.

"You must have boarded while we were visiting Stonehenge," said Thérèse-Anne.

"Yes, that is where we went back to the coach," said Penelope. "But where are our parents?"

"They must be on the right *autobus*, back at Stonehenge," said Marie.

"Oh, no!" cried Harold. "We must go back! Our parents will think we have wandered off. We will be in so much trouble!"

At that moment the coach stopped. A tall lady stood up and said, "Now, children. We have arrived at Salisbury Cathedral. We will spend the afternoon here. Remember to always stay together with the group. And ask me if you need any English words explained."

"That is our teacher, *Mademoiselle* Linnet," said Jean-Claude. "She planned this trip through England to practice our English."

"Maybe she can help you to find your parents," said Marie.

Chapter Seven

Salisbury Cathedral

Harold and Penelope followed their new friends off the coach. They went into Salisbury Cathedral. They were careful to tiptoe. So no one would realize there were elephants in the Cathedral.

Mademoiselle Linnet was busy explaining English phrases. She clearly knew a lot about Salisbury Cathedral. So Harold and Penelope waited quietly to speak to her.

"Look at this clock, Penelope," said Harold. "It is

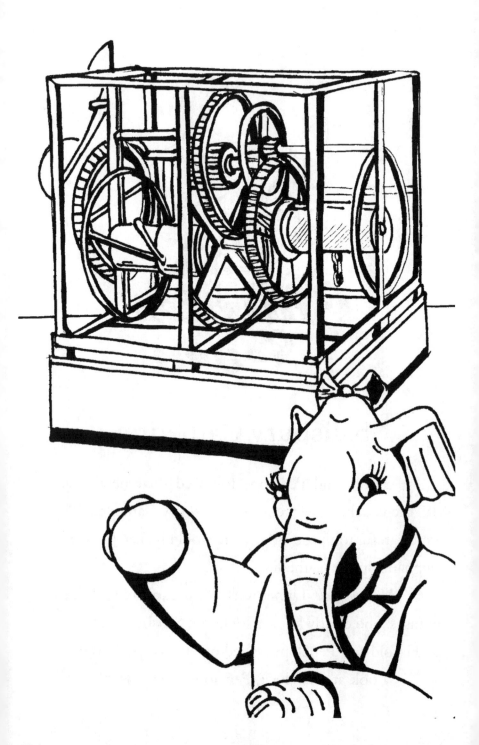

the oldest working clock in Europe! It was built back in 1386."

"Wow," said Penelope. "Nothing in Elephas is that old!"

"Except for your dinosaurs," said Harold.

"We will now visit the Chapter House," said *Mademoiselle* Linnet. "The Cathedral has a copy of the Magna Carta. It is one of only four left from 1215!"

"What is the Magna Carta?" Harold whispered to Penelope.

"Weren't you listening in class last week?" asked Penelope. "Or were you playing with your toy soldiers?"

"It is a very important piece of law," said *Mademoiselle* Linnet. "The constitutions of many countries are based on the Magna Carta. Such as the United States."

"And Elephas," whispered Penelope to Harold.

Mademoiselle Linnet noticed Harold and Penelope whispering.

"Wait a minute," said *Mademoiselle* Linnet. "I do not recognize you two. You are not students of mine, *non?*"

"No, *Mademoiselle* Linnet," said Harold. "We got on your coach by mistake at Stonehenge. We should be with another tour group."

"We do not want our parents to be worried," said

Penelope.

"*Mon dieu,*" said *Mademoiselle* Linnet. "We must find your parents, *immediatement!*"

"Speak English only, *Mademoiselle* Linnet!" reminded her students.

Mademoiselle Linnet led everyone back to the tour coach. The driver took them to the coach center.

The coach driver telephoned the tour company. He explained the situation.

He then turned to *Mademoiselle* Linnet. He said, "Their parents have already spoken to the company. They were sent to Salisbury Cathedral to look for you there!"

"*Oo, la la,*" said *Mademoiselle* Linnet. "We must have missed your parents at the Cathedral. We must return there, *immediatement!*"

So, the coach driver drove back to Salisbury Cathedral.

Chapter Eight

"Do you have a convertible?"

Mr. and Mrs. Elephant rode to Salisbury Cathedral in the coach. When they arrived, they went to the ticket desk.

"Have you seen a group of French students?" asked Mr. Elephant.

"Why yes," said the desk clerk, "They came in a little while ago. They went that direction with their teacher," he pointed.

"Oh, thank you," said Mrs. Elephant.

Mr. and Mrs. Elephant tiptoed quickly through the Cathedral. They stopped often to ask if anyone had seen the French students. And the attendants helpfully pointed them in the right direction.

Mr. and Mrs. Elephant entered the Chapter House. Mr. Elephant asked an attendant about the French students.

"Oh, yes," said the attendant. "They went out that door. I think they drove away in a coach."

"Oh, no!" cried Mrs. Elephant. "We have missed them! Whatever will happen to my babies?"

"Now, now, my dear," said Mr. Elephant. "They must be driving to their next stop. Our driver knows where they were going to next."

"Hmmm," said Colin as he studied his notes. "The company said the French group drives to Bristol tonight. Then they spend tomorrow in Glastonbury and Avebury."

"Then we must go to Bristol," said Mr. Elephant.

"I am afraid that I cannot take you there," said Colin.

"Why not?" asked Mrs. Elephant. She began to cry.

"I would like to help you find your children," said Colin. "But I have to take this tour group to Portsmouth tonight. And Bristol is in the wrong direction."

"Oh, no, what shall we do?" sobbed Mrs. Elephant. Mr. Elephant patted her shoulder.

"I saw a place where you can hire a car. You could drive to Bristol and find your children," said Colin.

Mr. and Mrs. Elephant agreed this was a good idea. Colin took them to the car hire agency. "I know you will find your children," he said. "And I am sorry that I cannot help you any more."

"Thank you so much for all of your help. I do not know what we would have done," said Mrs. Elephant.

Mr. and Mrs. Elephant went into the car hire agency. "I would like to hire a car to drive to Bristol. The name is Elefant. E-L-E-F-A-N-T," said Mr. Elephant.

"Certainly, Mr. Elefant," said the car hire agent. "Hmmm...Elefant...Elefant... That is an unusual name. Is it French?"

"No," said Mr. Elephant, in a tired voice.

"Now, then, Mr. Elefant. What sort of car would you like?" asked the agent.

Mr. Elephant considered this for a moment. "A large one," he said.

"I am sorry, Mr. Elefant," said the car hire agent. "I have just checked our computer. The only cars we have today are Mini Coopers. Would one of those be okay?"

Mr. Elephant looked at Mrs. Elephant. He saw how worried she was. "Do you have a convertible Mini?" asked Mr. Elephant.

"We have one with a sunroof," said the car hire agent.

"We will take it," said Mr. Elephant. He hoped that they could squeeze into the Mini.

The car hire agent gave the Elephants a map. And he wrote down directions to Bristol. Mr. and Mrs. Elephant squeezed into the Mini, and drove away. (They were both very glad for the sunroof.)

Chapter Nine

Bristol

The French tour group arrived back at Salisbury Cathedral on the coach. *Mademoiselle* Linnet told her students to stay on the coach. She went inside with Harold and Penelope.

The three of them rushed up to the desk attendant. "Have you seen our parents?" asked Harold.

"They have rather large noses, and large ears," said Penelope.

"And they were wearing raincoats and carrying

umbrellas," added Harold.

"Why yes," said the attendant. "They went that direction. I think they were looking for you."

"Thank you, thank you!" said Penelope.

Mademoiselle Linnet, Harold, and Penelope dashed through the Cathedral.

They arrived back at the Chapter House. They asked the attendant if he had seen their parents.

"Why yes," said the attendant. "I told them that I saw you drive away. They were going to follow you to your next stop."

"Oh, that is good to hear," said *Mademoiselle* Linnet. "Your parents will be waiting for us in Bristol. We will drive to our hotel and meet them there."

Mademoiselle Linnet, Harold, and Penelope got back on the coach. The driver took them to their hotel in Bristol.

The children all had fun on the drive. Harold asked his new friends many questions about French food. "*Comment dit-on en français* ice cream?" asked Harold.

"*La crème glacée!*" said Pierre.

They arrived at their hotel in Bristol. But Mr. and Mrs. Elephant were not there.

It was time for dinner. *Mademoiselle* Linnet asked

Harold and Penelope to join her students. They all went to the hotel café.

"Now, children," said *Mademoiselle* Linnet as their dinners were served. "We will eat the traditional English meal we have read about. Fish and chips!"

"Yay!" cheered all the children.

"I have never eaten Fish and Chips before," said Marie. "Is it, how you say, yummy?"

"Very yummy!" said Penelope. Penelope and Harold were pleased that their meals were served with peas. Because (as most everyone knows by now) elephants are very fond of peas.

The children were all very tired after their adventures that day. *Mademoiselle* Linnet led them to the extra large bedroom. It was lined on both sides with beds. The girls would all sleep on one side of the room. And the boys would all sleep on the other side.

Mademoiselle Linnet found extra pajamas and toothbrushes for Harold and Penelope. The children each took a bath. They changed into their pajamas, and brushed their teeth.

Then *Mademoiselle* Linnet tucked each child into bed. And kissed them all goodnight.

Mademoiselle Linnet tucked in Harold and Penelope.

She said, "Sleep well tonight. I know your parents will be here in the morning."

Harold and Penelope both fell asleep. They dreamed of finding their parents.

Chapter Ten

Mademoiselle Linnet's Plan

Mr. and Mrs. Elephant arrived in Bristol that evening. Mrs. Elephant said, "Oh, no! We forgot to ask for the name of the hotel! How will we ever find Harold and Penelope now?"

Mr. Elephant thought for a moment. "We must go to every hotel. We will ask if French students are staying there."

Mr. and Mrs. Elephant walked into the first hotel. They asked if French students were staying there. The

desk clerk told them no.

They then went to the second hotel. They asked if French students were staying there. The desk clerk told them no. So they went to the third hotel.

They kept looking for their children until it was very late. And they still had not found Harold and Penelope.

Mr. Elephant looked at his watch. "Harold and Penelope must be in bed by now," he said. "Let's spend the night at this hotel. We will continue looking in the morning."

Mrs. Elephant was still very worried about her children. "I hate to be parted from my babies. Even if it is just for one night. But I am certain the teacher will take good care of them."

"Yes," said Mr. Elephant. "I am certain Harold and Penelope will not be too much trouble. And we will find them in the morning."

"Oh, I certainly hope so," said Mrs. Elephant. "I miss them so much!"

Mr. and Mrs. Elephant both took a bath. They changed into their pajamas, and brushed their teeth. They both missed being able to kiss Harold and Penelope goodnight. They went to sleep. And dreamed about finding their children in the morning.

* * *

The next morning, Harold and Penelope woke up with the French students. *"Bon matin, mes amis!"* called out Thérèse-Anne.

"English only," reminded *Mademoiselle* Linnet.

"Good morning to you, too," called Penelope to Thérèse-Anne.

The children all dressed in their school uniforms. They rode the lift down to the hotel café.

"And now, children," said *Mademoiselle* Linnet. "We will taste the Full English Breakfast we have read about."

"Yay!" cried the children as their breakfasts were served.

Harold and Penelope were both pleased to see everything on their plates. There were sausages, eggs, bacon, tomatoes, mushrooms, baked beans, and black pudding.

"I wonder where Mummy and Daddy are," said Penelope. She stirred milk and sugar into her tea. "Breakfast without them is not the same."

"You are right," said Harold. "I wonder why they have not found us yet." He sounded a little worried.

After breakfast, *Mademoiselle* Linnet took the children back to their room. The French students packed their suitcases. *Mademoiselle* Linnet took Harold and Penelope aside.

"Your parents must be having some trouble finding us," she said. "But I have thought of a plan. We will leave a note for your parents. I will tell them exactly where we are going next."

"Our tour will pass through London before we return to Paris. We will drop you off there. If your parents do not catch up with us. I will tell your parents this in the note. And I will tell them not to worry," she added.

Harold and Penelope had been sad to not find their parents. But now they both felt cheered up.

They could spend more time with their new friends. And they would soon find their parents.

Chapter Eleven

King Arthur's Court

Harold and Penelope climbed aboard the coach with the other students. Penelope sat with her new friends Marie and Thérèse-Anne.

Harold sat with his new friends Jean-Claude and Pierre. Pierre shared sweets with Harold and Jean-Claude. Harold had to remember to call them *"les bon-bons."*

Here we are at the ruins of Glastonbury Abbey," said *Mademoiselle* Linnet. "This was once the greatest church in the middle ages. Please remember to show your respect."

The children were all happy to see the Abbey ruins. "Wow," said Harold. "There is the grave of King Arthur and Queen Guinevere!"

"People say that Glastonbury was really Avalon," said Penelope. "I wonder where Camelot is?"

"Do you think they still have King Arthur's round table?" asked Harold

"Can you imagine what this looked like centuries ago?" asked Penelope.

"Can you believe these walls have not fallen down?" said Harold.

Marie-Claire added, "*Mademoiselle* Linnet says that the Holy Grail is buried nearby."

"Penelope is going to be an archaeologist," said Harold. "She could find the Holy Grail."

"Well," said Penelope, "I might look for it. But only if there were dinosaur bones to dig up, too."

They visited the Abbot's kitchen. A man dressed as a monk told them about cooking at the abbey.

"The monks were vegetarians. They ate very simple meals," he said. "But the Abbot and his guests ate meat and drank wine." He showed them models of how the food would have been cooked.

Harold groaned and rubbed his tummy. "Why

does all the food have to be pretend? I am hungry for real food!"

Mademoiselle Linnet took everyone to a nice pub for lunch. They all ate more fish and chips for lunch.

"I must ask my mother to cook fish and chips," said Jean-Claude.

Harold and Penelope were pleased that their meals were served with peas. Because (as all good students know) elephants are very fond of peas.

The tour coach then took them to Avebury. This stone circle was so big that most of the village was inside it.

The children were very happy they could walk around the stone circle. They could even touch the stones.

"Wow," said Penelope. "This stone circle is even older than Stonehenge."

"And it is so much bigger!" said Harold

"I like this much better than Stonehenge," added Penelope. She and Harold climbed on a low stone. "All I remember of Stonehenge is how my tummy hurt."

"I wonder if we can see Mummy and Daddy from here," added Harold. He had begun to worry about their parents.

"I am certain they will find us," said Penelope. "*Mademoiselle* Linnet left a note with really good directions."

Harold and Penelope held hands as they looked at the large stones. They both hoped to see their parents soon.

Chapter Twelve

Mrs. Elephant's Idea

Mr. and Mrs. Elephant woke up in their hotel. They immediately thought about finding Harold and Penelope. They dressed quickly, putting on their raincoats over their clothes. With their disguises, no one would guess that they were elephants.

Mr. and Mrs. Elephant checked out of their hotel

without eating breakfast. Which shows how worried they were about Harold and Penelope. Both Mr. and Mrs. Elephant were quite fond of Full English Breakfasts.

Mr. Elephant said, "We must hurry. We have so many hotels to check. We do not want to miss Harold and Penelope again."

"Wait, dear," said Mrs. Elephant. "I have an idea. If we keep driving around, they may leave before we get there."

"Let's ring the coach company," continued Mrs. Elephant. "They can tell us where the French students are staying."

"That is an excellent idea, my dear!" said Mr. Elephant. "That will save us a lot of time."

Mrs. Elephant telephoned the coach company. She learned where the French students were staying.

Mr. and Mrs. Elephant climbed into the Mini Cooper. They drove to the hotel and rushed inside.

Mr. Elephant rushed up to the desk clerk. "Is there a group of French students here?" he asked.

The desk clerk said, "Ah, yes. You must be Mr. and Mrs. Elefant. What an unusual name. Is it French?"

"No," said Mr. Elephant. "Are our children here?"

"No, I am afraid that they left earlier this morning.

With the French tour group," said the desk clerk.

"Oh, no! We are too late again!" cried Mrs. Elephant.

"Do not worry Mrs. Elefant," said the desk clerk. "The teacher left a note for you. She wrote down the stops the tour will make. And the addresses of all their hotels."

Mr. and Mrs. Elephant thanked the desk clerk. They went to the sitting room to read the note.

"Their next stop is the ruins of Glastonbury Abbey," said Mr. Elephant. He looked at his watch. "We must hurry. Then we can catch them before they leave."

"No, dear," said Mrs. Elephant. "I have a better idea. If we go to Glastonbury, we might miss them again. Let's go to the hotel where they will be staying tonight."

"An excellent idea, my dear!" said Mr. Elephant. "We will be waiting for them when they arrive."

"Let's see," said Mrs. Elephant. "They spend tonight at a hotel in Woodstock. And visit Blenheim Palace tomorrow."

Mr. and Mrs. Elephant squeezed back into the Mini Cooper. They drove to the village of Woodstock. They found the hotel where the French students would be staying. Then they sat down to wait in the hotel lobby.

While they waited, Mrs. Elephant said, "This is a

lovely place. We should take Harold and Penelope to visit Blenheim Palace tomorrow."

"The home of Winston Churchill," said Mr. Elephant. "I have always wanted to go there."

"Another great diplomat, just like my wonderful husband," said Mrs. Elephant. She leaned over and kissed his cheek.

"Oh, I am not a great diplomat," said Mr. Elephant. He blushed a little. But he was very proud that she felt that way.

Chapter Thirteen

Bangers and Mash

The coach parked in front of the hotel in Woodstock. Harold and Penelope were very sad that they had not found their parents yet. Harold said, "What if we never see Mummy and Daddy again? Will we have to go to school in Paris?"

"Don't be silly," said Penelope. "*Mademoiselle* Linnet

left a note for them. She told them exactly where we will be. And she said she would drop us off in London. If Mummy and Daddy do not catch up with us."

"Well, that is good," said Harold, with a sigh. "I don't know if I can ever learn when to use *le* or *la.*"

"Look, look!" cried Penelope. "There are Mummy and Daddy. They are waving their umbrellas at us!"

Harold and Penelope rushed into the arms of their parents. Mr. and Mrs. Elephant hugged them both tightly.

"Oh, Daddy, please do not be cross with us," said Harold.

"We got on the wrong coach by mistake," said Penelope.

"We were so worried you would not find us. And we would have to go live in Paris. And learn French. And Mummy, I just don't know when to use *le* or *la*!" Harold said this all in one big breath.

"Do not worry," said Mr. Elephant with a laugh. "Your mother knew exactly how to find you. It just took us a little longer than we thought."

"Come meet our new friends, and *Mademoiselle* Linnet," said Penelope. "She was very nice to us."

"Thank you so much, *Mademoiselle* Linnet," said Mr.

and Mrs. Elephant. "For taking such good care of our children. And for your excellent directions to the hotel. We do not know how else we would have found you."

"It was a pleasure to have them with us," said *Mademoiselle* Linnet. "They have helped my students to practice their English. And Harold has told us so much about English food. We would love you to join us at dinner tonight. I have read that the café here serves delicious Bangers and Mash."

"We would love to have dinner with you. And meet Harold and Penelope's new friends," said Mr. Elephant.

Everyone sat down for an excellent dinner of Bangers and Mash. Harold explained that he had not yet been served firecrackers. But he kept hoping that someday he would.

The Elephants were pleased that their food was served with peas. Because (as everyone in England knows) elephants are very fond of *les petits pois*.

What the Elephants Saw in England

City of Bath

      Roman Baths

      Bath Abbey

      Pulteney Bridge

Stonehenge Monument

Salisbury Cathedral

Glastonbury Abbey Ruins

Stone Circle at Avebury

What the Elephants Ate in England

Fish and chips

Shepherd's Pie

Cornish Pasty

Bangers and Mash

Tea with milk and sugar

Bath buns

Sally Lunn buns

Spa water at the Pump House in the Roman Baths

Cider

Full English Breakfast: eggs, sausages, bacon, baked beans, tomatoes, mushrooms, and black pudding

...and, of course, peas! Because (as everyone in England knows) elephants are very fond of peas.

The Elephants' Guide to British Terms:

pocket money = allowance

holiday = vacation

coach = a bus that travels to different cities

Union flag = sometimes called the Union Jack, the
national flag of the United Kingdom

sweet = candy

lift = elevator

chemist = pharmacy

petrol = gasoline

coach center = bus station

to hire a car = to rent a car

to ring = to call on the telephone

The Elephants' Guide to British Food:

Fish and chips = fried fish and French fries

Bath bun = small, round bun that is very sweet

Sally Lunn bun = a type of tea cake, it can be eaten with sweet or savory toppings

Spa Water = water from the hot springs in the Roman baths

Shepherd's pie = a lamb stew cooked in a piecrust with mashed potatoes on top

Cornish pasty = beef and potatoes in a piecrust that is eaten without a fork

Bangers and mash = sausages and mashed potatoes

Black pudding = a sausage made with beef blood and other fillings

The Elephants' Guide to Speaking French:

Bonjour = hello

Parlez-vous français? = Do you speak French?

non = no

oui = yes

Je m'appelle ____ = My name is _____

Et vous êtes elephants = And you are elephants

Nous ne sommes pas éléphants = We are not elephants

aussi = also

pourquoi? = why?

Et c'est ma soeur = And this is my sister

Il est très stupide = He is very stupid

autobus = bus, coach

Mademoiselle = Miss

Mon dieu! = My goodness!

immediatement = immediately

Comment dit-on en français ice cream? = How do you say in French ice cream?

la crème glacée = ice cream

Bon matin, mes amis! = Good morning, my friends!

les bon-bons = candy, sweets

les petits pois = peas

Help the Elephants Plan Their Next Vacation!

Where would you like to see the Elephant family visit next?

Please email the Elephant Family at:
elephants@simplyelephants.com
(Always get your parents' permission before going on-line!)

Or send a post card to:
The Elephant Family
Kinkajou Press
9 Mockingbird Hill Road
Tijeras, New Mexico 87059

You can learn more about the Elephant Family and their adventures at: www.simplyelephants.com

Dear Elephant Family,

I would like to see you visit _____

_____

_____

I think that you would have fun there because _____

_____

_____

_____

Things that I liked about your adventures in England were

_____

_____

_____

Your friend,

_____

_____

_____

Free Elephant Family Fan Club

Want to keep up with all of the Elephant Family's adventures? Join the free Elephant Family Fan Club!

See where the Elephants are traveling to next. Register for e-mail greetings from Harold and Penelope, and more! Be the first to find out about the next Elephant Family book, *The Elephants in the Land of Enchantment.* Buy Elephant Family books and gifts.

All new fan club members will receive a free gift from the Elephant Family.

Sign up on-line at: www.simplyelephants.com
(Always get your parents' permission before going on-line!)

Or send a postcard: Kinkajou Press

9 Mockingbird Hill Road

Tijeras, New Mexico 87059

Coming Soon!

The Elephants in the Land of Enchantment

An Adventure in Albuquerque!

The Elephant family travels to America to visit their friend Maria in New Mexico. Fun is in store as the Elephants enjoy New Mexican food, party at a *quinceañera* and visit the famous Albuquerque International Balloon Fiesta. Harold can't wait to see all the cowboys and Indians!

Maria has a special surprise waiting for the Elephant family. Can Harold and Penelope guess what it is? And will Harold find any chili he doesn't like?

Get ready for a great adventure with the Elephant family!

Beverly Eschberger enjoys writing books she would have liked to read as a child. These books include *The Elephant Family Adventure* series, and several other books soon to be published.

Ms. Eschberger lives in New Mexico with her husband and son. She first met the Elephant Family on a trip to Bath, England, and has been traveling the world with them ever since. She is working on the next books in *The Elephant Family Adventure* series.

Order Form

Elephant Family Adventures

_____   The Elephants Visit London ($3.99 ea.)
_____   The Elephants Tour England ($3.99 ea.)
_____   The Elephants in the Land of Enchantment ($3.99 ea.)

_____   Total Number of Books _____ Total Cost
_____   I would like my copy autographed by Beverly
          Eschberger!

My Check or Money Order for $ _____ is enclosed.
Please charge my _____ Visa _____ MC

Name: _____

Address: _____

City: _____

State: _____ Zip: _____

Email: _____

Phone: _____

Credit Card #: _____

Exp Date: _____ CCV# _____
                                  (3 digit # on back of card)

Mail to: Artemesia Publishing
        9 Mockingbird Hill Rd
        Tijeras, New Mexico 87059
Or Call: 1-505-286-0892
Or visit us online at: www.apbooks.net